MR. BOUNCER'S HOUSE

FIRE STATION

BLODGER'S GATEHOUSE

SIGMUND SWAMP'S HOUSE & BOATHOUSE

FERNYBANK FERRY

BROCK GRUFFY'S SHOP

BRAMBLE'S FARM

CHURCH

VICARAGE

RAILWAY STATION

P.C. HOPPIT'S HOUSE

POLICE STATION

DR. BUSHY'S HOUSE

N
W · E
S

This book belongs to:

....

PUBLISHED BY PETER HADDOCK LIMITED, BRIDLINGTON, ENGLAND.
© FERN HOLLOW PRODUCTIONS LIMITED.

SPIKE AND THE
COWBOY BAND

Written & Illustrated by John Patience

Spike Willowbank was on his way to see Sigmund Swamp for his music lesson. Spike played the violin and was looking forward to performing in the Fern Hollow Music Festival later that week. The hedgehog turned a corner in the lane and was surprised by a couple of his friends who were racing down the hill in their billycarts and almost knocked him over. "Hello, Spike!" said Patch. "Come and play on the carts with us." "Sorry, I can't," said Spike. "I have to go to my music lesson." "Yuck!" said Patch. "Music is boring." "Yes," agreed Monty. "Billycarts are much more fun!" Spike wondered if his friends might be right, but he continued on his way to Sigmund's house.

"Good morning, Spike," said Sigmund. "Are you looking forward to the Music Festival?" "Oh yes, of course!" replied Spike, though by now he was not so sure. "Jolly good," said the toad. "Let me hear the piece you've been practising." Spike began to play but, after a time, his concentration was broken by a loud snoring noise. He glanced across at Sigmund and discovered that he had fallen fast asleep. "Oh dear," sighed Spike. "This must be a very boring piece of music if it sends the teacher to sleep!"

At Trundleberry Manor the Fern Hollow Brass Band was practising their contribution to the Music Festival. "Yes, that was very good," said Lord Trundle when the band had stopped playing. "I think the festival will be a great success. As well as the band there will be all the other contributions: Mr Periwinkle will play his flute; there will be the recorder group and Spike Willowbank will play his violin." "I agree," said Brock Gruffy. "It will be very entertaining, but it would be nice if we could think of something to make it a little different this year." "Mmmm, you're right," said Lord Trundle. "Listen, I think I have an idea."

The next day Spike and his friends were fishing in the River Ferny when Jingle's taxi drew up close by at the Jolly Vole Hotel. They all watched as Jingle opened the door for his passengers and they stepped out. They were four animals dressed like cowboys. One of them, a raccoon, tipped Jingle and then they all disappeared into the hotel. "Wow!" cried Patch. "They look great. I wonder if they're real cowboys."

That night as Spike lay in bed he heard music drifting across from the Jolly Vole. It was the sort of music that cowboys play. "Of course," said Spike, "they are a Cowboy Band. That's wonderful!" Spike was very excited. He crept out of the house and ran down the lane to the hotel. The music was coming from one of the upstairs rooms. Spike clambered up a tree and peeped in through the window.

The band was practising. They sounded marvellous! The music was very jolly, the sort of thing that would make you want to dance. In fact, Spike began to rock and jiggle around in the tree. That was a mistake because suddenly the hedgehog lost his balance and fell. Fortunately, his pyjamas caught on a branch and he was left dangling high above the ground. "Help!" cried Spike. "Somebody get me down!" The landlord of the Jolly Vole and the Cowboy Band quickly came rushing out to see what all the noise was about. "Don't worry, pardner!" shouted Rip, the bandleader. "I'll get you down!" Rip at once began to shin up the tree.

He climbed out on to the branch on which Spike was caught and pulled him up. Everyone cheered, but the next moment there was a loud crack, the branch broke and they both fell down to the ground! Spike was all right – he landed on top of Rip, who broke his fall – but the raccoon himself was not so lucky. He had badly hurt one arm. Doctor Bushy came and put it in a sling. "I'm afraid you won't be able to play the fiddle for a while," he said. "Darn it," said Rip. "Lord Trundle invited us here to play in your Music Festival. What are we going to do now?" "I can play the violin," said Spike. "Perhaps you could teach me some of your music and I could be in the Cowboy Band." "Well, I guess we could try it," agreed Rip.

The next day was Music Festival day. Mr Chips, the carpenter, had built a little bandstand in one of Farmer Bramble's fields. The Fern Hollow Brass Band played their music there all afternoon.

Later, in the evening, came the special event – the Barn Dance. "And now," cried Lord Trundle, "I give you Spike and the Cowboy Band!" Spike had managed to learn the music. Though Rip couldn't play his fiddle he could still call for the dances and the Fern Hollow animals had a real hoe-down! You can just imagine how impressed Spike's friends were! They certainly never said anything about music being boring, ever again!

Fern Hollow

MR CHIPS'S HOUSE

MR WILLOWBANK'S
COBBLER'S SHOP

MR CROAKER'S WATERMILL

STRIPEY'S HOUSE

SCHOOL

THE JOLLY VOLE
HOTEL

RIVER FERNY

MR ACORN'S
BAKERY

MR RUSTY'S HOUSE

POST OFFICE

BORIS BLINKS'S
BOOKSHOP

MR PRICKLES'S HOUSE

MR TWINKLE'S
HOUSE

MR TUTTLEBEE'S
SHOP

MR THIMBLE'S
TAILOR'S SHOP

WINDYWOOD